For my mom, Marjorie Fisher, who gave me dreams
For Mark, who is the best thing that ever happened to me,
and for Sam and Stephanie, our double blessings
—M. O.

Margaret K. McElderry Books
An imprint of Simon & Schuster Children's Publishing Division
1230 Avenue of the Americas, New York, New York 10020
Text copyright © 2003 by Margaret O'Hair
Illustrations copyright © 2003 by Thierry Courtin
Book design by Ann Bobco and Kristin Smith
The text for this book is set in Rotis Serif.
The illustrations are rendered as digital art.
Manufactured in China
2 4 6 8 10 9 7 5 3 1
Library of Congress Cataloging-in-Publication Data
O'Hair, Margaret.
Twin to twin / by Margaret O'Hair ; illustrated by Thierry Courtin.— 1st ed.
p. cm.
Summary: A rhyming description of the
characteristics and activities of twin toddlers.
ISBN 0-689-84494-8
[1. Twins—Fiction. 2. Toddlers—Fiction. 3. Day—Fiction. 4. Stories in rhyme.]
I. Courtin, Thierry, ill. II. Title.
PZ8.3.O353 Tw 2003
[E]—dc21
2001031723

FIRST
EDITION

Twin to Twin

WRITTEN BY margaret o'hair ❁ ILLUSTRATED BY thierry courtin

Margaret K. McElderry Books New York London Toronto Sydney Singapore

Double born.
Twice the blessing.

Double kids.
Twice the messing.

Double babies'
blankies, binkies.

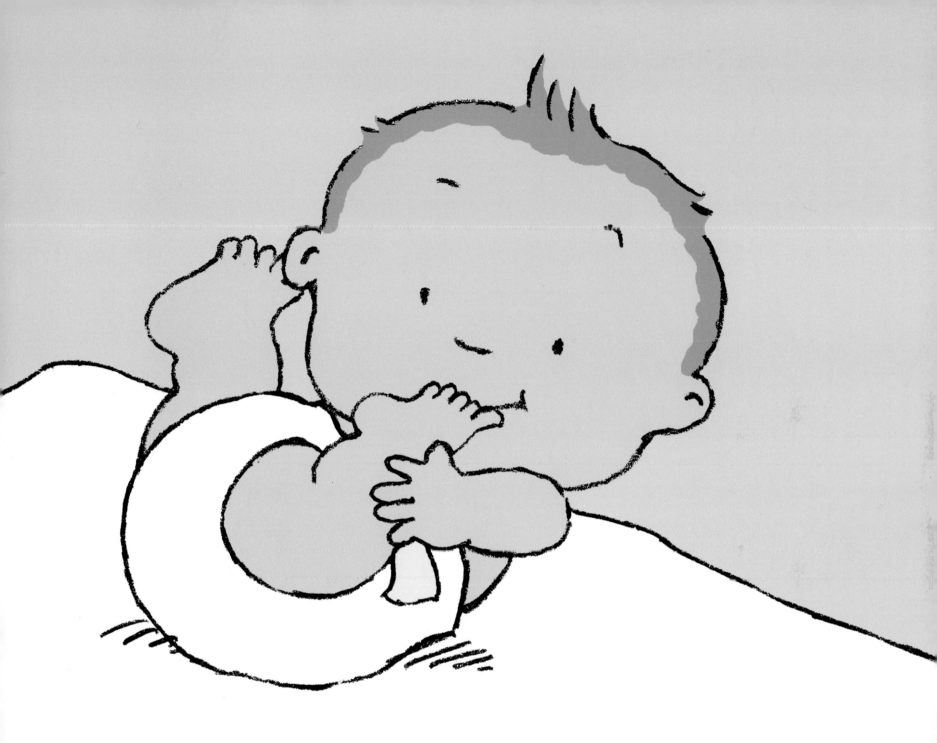

Double diapers,
clean or stinkies.

Double crawl,
then double walk.

Conversation,
double talk!

Double giggles
when they're glad.

Double tantrums
when they're mad.

Double love.
Double hugs.

Double catch
the lady bugs.

Double feed
the yellow ducks.

Double roll
toy cars and trucks.

Double ride
the shaggy pony.

Double cheese
and macaroni!

Double kites
on a string.

High and low
on the swing.

Double singing

where they go—

"Eee aye eee aye eee aye oh!"

Double rolling
down the hill.

Double Band-Aids
when they spill.

Double shirts.
Double jeans.

Belly buttons
in between.

Double splashing
in the tub.

Double bubbles.
Double scrub.

Double brushing
shiny teeth.

Double monster.
Check underneath!

Double dance.
Double smile.

Double jump.
Pillow pile!

Mirror double.
Peek and see.

Am I you?

Or are you me?

Double hold
their teddy bears.

Double kisses,
hugs, and prayers.

Double tired
from all their play.

Double dreams
for their next day.

Double hands,
skin to skin.

Double hearts,
twin to twin.